A FOREST OF PIPES
The Story of the Walt Disney Concert Hall Organ

Jennifer Zobelein

Introduction by Jonathan Ambrosino

BALCONY PRESS   LOS ANGELES

To my husband, Craig—my favorite
musician and the greatest supporter
of this project.

First Edition
Published in the United States of
America by Balcony Press 2007

Design by Distinc

Pre-press and production by
Navigator Cross-media, Pasadena, CA

A FOREST OF PIPES
© 2007 Jennifer Zobelein

Library of Congress Catalogue
Card Number: 2006935743
ISBN: 978-1-890449-43-8

The author is indebted to those who
provided the many photographs used
in this book. The great majority of them
were supplied through the courtesy
of Glatter-Götz Orgelbau and Rosales
Organ Builders.

Other sources are listed below.

Lawrence Bartone: cover photo,
and photos pages 26, 31, 32, 64

Ron Belanger: photo page 10

Rick Flynn: photo page 72

Gehry Partners: photos pages 8, 14;
sketches pages 16, 17; CATIA models
pages 10, 11; scale models pages 14, 18,
19, 20, 21, 33

Jim Lewis: photo page 22

Gavin Martin: photo page 67

Grant Mudford: photo pages 62 (top), 71

Robert Tall: photo page 59 (top-right),
page 60 (4th down on left), page 60
(2nd down on right), and page 70

CONTENTS

PREFACE

The Walt Disney Concert Hall is a sculptured building. Designed by architect Frank O. Gehry, it opened in Los Angeles in the fall of 2003. Its gleaming metallic exterior rises in undulating curves and slanted walls, in shapes reminiscent of sturdy ships and billowing sails. Inside this signature building is a perfectly symmetrical auditorium with terraced seating encircling the platform. Within this intimate hall of light and color, the startling organ façade is the dramatic and visual focus — towering above the rear of the stage as a *forest of pipes.*

Incorporating an organ into the design of an auditorium is difficult at best and Frank Gehry devoted a great deal of time to its appearance and placement. It was clear that he did not want a conventional organ with the pipes lined up in a neat symmetrical array. Something of compelling interest was required to match the ingenuity of the building. He insisted on designing the arrangement of the façade pipes himself.

The person selected to consult with Gehry was Manuel J. Rosales, a Los Angeles organ designer and builder. It was his purpose to define the parameters for Gehry and agree upon a design which would allow the architectural expression desired, but also accommodate the mechanical and tonal needs of the organ. Once this was established, Rosales searched for someone to fabricate and install the many complex components. His recommendation was Caspar von Glatter-Götz, a European organ builder whose company offered impressive technical competence,

as well as great enthusiasm. These three individuals, and their dedicated associates, produced a superb pipe organ, an instrument of great visual and tonal beauty. The entire process, from early design concepts to the finished product, stretched over fifteen years.

This book was written for people who delight in the imaginative, who yearn to understand the creative spirit, who appreciate the craftsmanship that produces a work of art. The author went to those most intimately acquainted with this pipe organ—to the architects, designers, builders and musicians. Indeed, their thoughts, words and insights provide the substance of this book. It is the author's intention to bring them the honor they deserve.

Jennifer Zobelein

L TO R:
ORGAN DESIGNER MANUEL J. ROSALES
ARCHITECT FRANK O. GEHRY
ORGAN BUILDER CASPAR VON GLATTER-GÖTZ

INTRODUCTION

In the 1950s, stereophonic technology and the long-playing record forever changed the listening experience. Edited performances of astonishing accuracy, played upon new high-fidelity equipment, placed unprecedented perfection and realism into the living room. In turn, listeners brought that expectation to the arena of live performance, both upping the bar for musicians and creating a fascination with perfecting the acoustical environment of the modern concert hall.

Many new halls at that time were furnished with pipe organs, not surprising in the era of superstar organists like Virgil Fox and E. Power Biggs. In the last two decades, however, further revolutions in recording and architectural acoustics brought dissatisfaction with the often arid sound of mid-20th-century symphony spaces. The organ's role as orchestral partner underwent a similar re-evaluation. Were the steely-sounding instruments of the 1950s and '60s really the proper match to the velvet of the Philadelphia strings or the bronze of the Cleveland brass? A turning point came in 1991 with the opening of the Meyerson Symphony Center in Dallas. Its adjustable acoustics gave clarity, warmth and reverberation, while its massive Fisk organ forever tabled the notion that a concert hall organ need only be a church instrument in black tie.

Los Angeles did not remain aloof from these trends. When new in 1964, the Dorothy Chandler Pavilion represented the last word in public performing arts centers, yet by the 1980s the public mindset had advanced to the point that a new symphony hall didn't seem farfetched. Then, as now, the new Walt Disney Concert Hall would have an organ, for which architect Frank Gehry made clear his starting point: if the Hall itself would bear little relation to traditional architecture, neither should its pipe organ assume a conventional appearance.

Thus began a gradual philosophical alignment between architect and organbuilder Manuel Rosales. The design evolved into an array of curved wooden pipes shooting out like Roman candle fireworks, some from the case, others from the floor of the Hall itself. A burst of brass trumpet pipes above the console would punctuate the appearance: a giant exclamation mark. The design earned immediate renegade status, much to Rosales' delight, for if people were fascinated by the instrument's appearance, wouldn't they be curious about its sound? Rosales ultimately invited the German firm of Glatter-Götz to build the organ in a collaborative venture, recognizing Caspar von Glatter-Götz's penchant for the unprecedented. Not only would an organ for Gehry's hall be the young firm's largest to date, Gehry's curved façade pipes would present an irresistible challenge.

Audiences immediately took to the bold, dashing sound, at once traditional and forward-looking. Solo organ recitals, those supposedly stodgy affairs, now sell out routinely. As Gehry hoped, the organ's appearance wasn't toned down or screened in, but crowned his design with an arresting thicket of pipes through which any visitor could amble in both fascination and awe — an enchanted forest, just like the best Walt Disney feature. What more ingenious launch for the American pipe organ in the 21st century?

Jonathan Ambrosino

FRANK O. GEHRY
Architect of the Walt Disney Concert Hall and Visual Designer of the Organ Façade

In 1987, Lillian Disney, widow of Walt Disney, offered a gift of $50 million toward the design and construction of a new auditorium in Los Angeles. An open competition was held for an architect with creative ideas for a new concert hall that would include a pipe organ. The jury found Frank Gehry's sketches and models unusual. Living in Southern California and owning a sailboat, Gehry was intrigued by the metaphorical implications. His design for the exterior of the building, as well as the interior of the hall, embraced the flowing lines and shapes of a ship under full sail — with the audience on board journeying through a sequence of musical adventures.

Though a recognized architect at that time, Gehry was considered something of a maverick and an outsider. He was known for his openly experimental designs of furniture and lamps, as well as buildings. His work was variously described as awkward, uneasy, and startling, as well as refreshingly original — even profound and brilliant. To the consternation of some and the delight of others, Frank Gehry's design was ultimately selected by the jury. It was the largest commission ever offered to him in his own city and it was his first concert hall. It was also his first organ façade design.

After consulting with Manuel J. Rosales, the organ builder originally selected for the project, he carefully studied about thirty different configurations. Could the organ be hung from the ceiling? Could the pipes be mounted upside down? Should they be hidden behind a movable screen? He came up with many options, but the designs were not always feasible. Gradually, over many months of discussion, he began to understand the possibilities as well as the limitations and saw an opportunity to create an organ unlike any seen before.

Ultimately, he chose Douglas fir to fashion enormous curved organ pipes, 32 feet long and of squared construction. These "speaking" pipes angle outward from the organ in a cohesive arrangement. Anchoring them was complex. Nothing quite so unusual and daring had been tried before. Preliminary drawings were made in 1991 including an earthquake-resistant structure for safety. Through collaboration with Manuel J. Rosales, the tonal designer of the organ, and Glatter-Götz organ builders in Germany, Gehry was able to integrate the organ into the architectural design of the hall. After more than fifteen years of work, the Walt Disney Concert Hall opened to international acclaim in the fall of 2003. The pipe organ was inaugurated one year later.

"Among his many accomplishments, Frank Gehry will be remembered as the architect who elevated the organ to be the magnificent center-piece of his design for the Walt Disney Concert Hall."
—MANUEL J. ROSALES, TONAL DESIGNER OF THE PIPE ORGAN

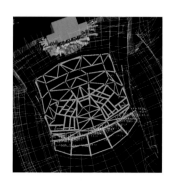

CATIA COMPUTER MODEL OF HALL AND ORGAN   WALT DISNEY CONCERT HALL

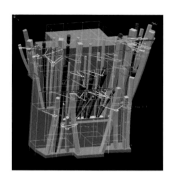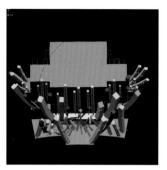

"The calculating and positioning of the braces for the façade pipes is a masterpiece of engineering — the reason being that all the braces had to reach the proper positions and not collide with each other, nor with any of the pipes." —Caspar von Glatter-Götz

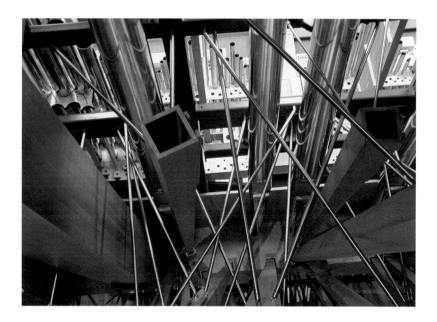

CATIA COMPUTER MODEL OF ORGAN　　　　THE COMPLEXITIES OF ACTUAL BRACING RODS

Toyota Motor Sales, USA, Inc. donated $3 million for the pipe organ to give Angelenos an instrument befitting their world-class concert hall.

Organist Todd Wilson at the main console, October, 2004.

EARLY DESIGN CONCEPT WITH DRAPED PIPES

CRAIG WEBB
Architect and Design Partner, Gehry Partners, LLP

JZ/ **Where did Gehry Partners begin in the conceptual design of this unique organ?** CW/ First of all, the Disney family specified that the organ should not have a church look, but should be appropriate for a concert hall. Manuel J. Rosales, the organ designer selected to work with us, wanted it to be in a case and with tracker action — that is, with mechanical links from the keys to the air valves of each pipe.

JZ/ **So, I suppose there had to be some discussion at the beginning, to explore the possibilities.** CW/ Yes, there was quite a didactic conversation about the philosophy of the design — just how much should be shown openly versus what should be hidden. Gehry suggested that the organ be placed behind doors or large panels that would open up when the organ was played. The inside of these doors could be decorated in Spanish style. However, Rosales resisted the thought that this important organ would be covered up. Finally, they both agreed that the organ should be part of the concert hall, not hidden away.

JZ/ **As I understand it, Gehry did not know a lot about organs, but his desire was to make a visual impact with an unusual design for the façade — the most visible pipes in the front of the organ case.** CW/ He started with the idea of a metal pipe façade. But metal pipes are soft, so arranging them at different angles would create a problem. Over a period of time, they would tend to sag and lose their shape. So Gehry examined the pipes inside an organ case and liked the look of the wooden ones. He suggested that they be placed outside the case and become the focal point of the façade. He was drawn to wood as a material he likes to work with, and also to match the wood inside the auditorium. There would be a "visual dialogue"

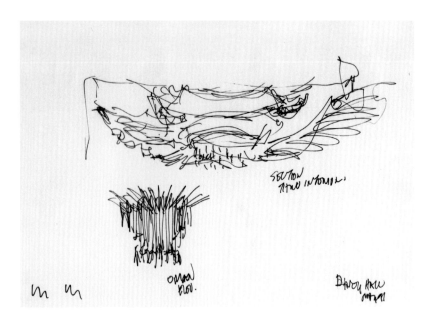

between the façade pipes and the hall. Later, he realized he could tilt these wooden pipes because of their strength.

JZ/ **What about size? There would have to be established parameters for the organ components.** CW/ Originally, the organ was to be an accompanying instrument for the orchestra. This idea was gradually upgraded to a solo instrument, also used for accompaniment. In architectural lingo, this is called scope creep! The organ definitely became more prominent as the design evolved — so of course it took up more space. It is also true that additional funds became available.

JZ/ **In reading about the design of the concert hall itself, I was impressed with the computer program, CATIA, that allows initial concepts to be transformed into actual working drawings. Can you tell me more about that?** CW/ Well, one of our partners, Jim Glymph, took a French aeronautical computer program used in building Mirage fighter jets and adapted it to Gehry's design method. After a wood model is made, based on a sketch, the Computer-Assisted Three-Dimensional Interactive Application scans the model and translates the information into drawings with detailed specifications for suppliers and builders. With the organ façade design, we were able to specify the exact dimensions,

FRANK GEHRY'S PRELIMINARY ORGAN CONCEPTS

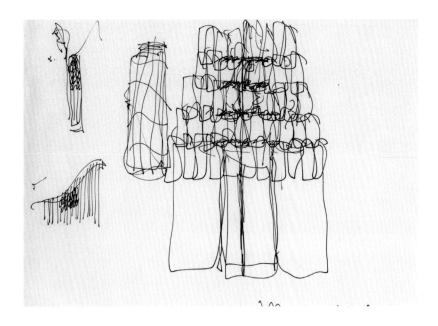

placement and angle of every pipe, brace and joint. This program allowed us to communicate electronically with Glatter-Götz Orgelbau in Germany, sending designs and specifications back and forth for the fabrication and installation of this complex organ façade. It also allowed us to analyze and adjust the egress of sound through the façade pipes to be sure the tones would be heard.

JZ/ **So, for each proposal, you were able to make sketches and models for Rosales to consider?** CW/ Yes, we produced 1:24 models — a half-inch scale — at first. Then for the acoustical tests, a 1:10 scale.

JZ/ **I noticed that some of the earlier models showed the horizontal pipes in a different position.** CW/ Gehry agreed that Rosales could add the enchamade of pipes, which became known as the Trompeta de Los Angeles, and also some brass to match the handrails in the hall. The horizontal trumpets were at first placed at the top of the case, but then lowered to their present position where they make a dramatic visual and tonal addition. The evolution of the whole organ façade design is really quite fascinating — and pleasing to the public.

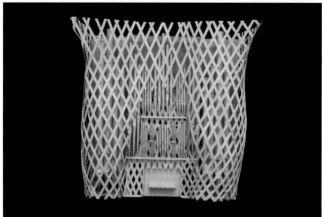

EARLY STUDY MODELS WERE QUITE DIFFERENT

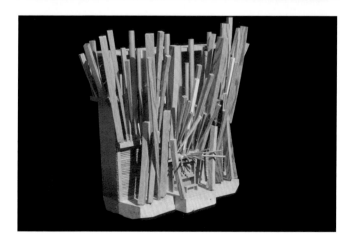

THEN IT BEGAN TO EVOLVE!

PIPES ARE STRAIGHT BUT ANGLED
TRUMPETS ARE AT THE TOP
TRUMPETS ARE BELOW

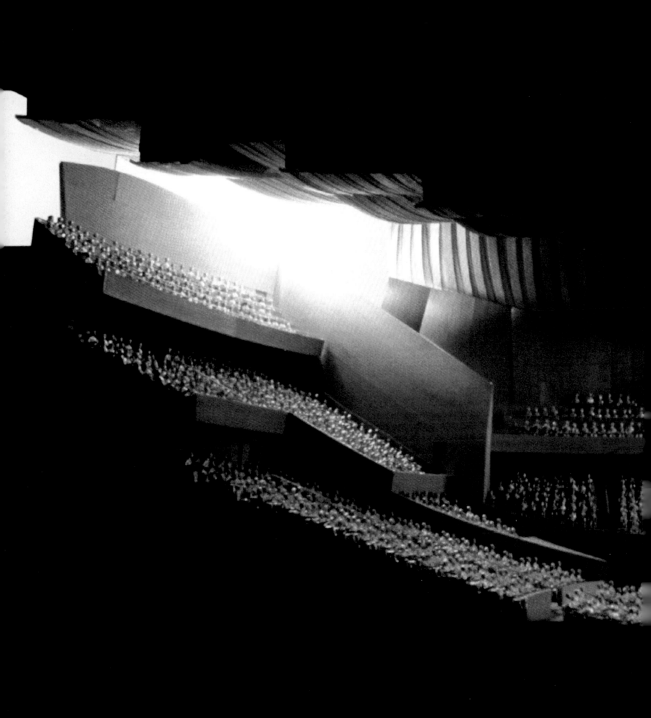

FINAL MODEL SHOWS THE PIPES IN THE CONTEXT OF THE HALL

J. MICHAEL BARONE

Organ Consultant for Walt Disney Concert Hall, Host and Producer of *Pipedreams* on National Public Radio

JZ/ **Can you tell me about the committee formed to select an organ designer and builder?** JMB/ At the beginning of the Walt Disney Concert Hall project, Ernest Fleischmann, then Managing Director of the L.A. Philharmonic, requested his Artistic Administrator, Ara Guzelimian (now Artistic Advisor to Carnegie Hall), to convene a small group to provide input on the matter of a pipe organ for the new space. Ara invited three prominent organists to participate: Cherry Rhodes, Adjunct Professor of Organ, and Ladd Thomas, Professor of Music and Chair of the Organ Department, both from the Thornton School of Music at the University of Southern California; and, Robert Anderson, Professor of Organ from Southern Methodist University. All of them had strong recitalist credentials. Two of them represented the Los Angeles perspective, and one of them, Dr. Anderson, had already gone through a similar process in Dallas as advisor for the Meyerson

Symphony Center, which set a new standard for a modern concert hall with pipe organ. My role was multi-faceted: a tutored enthusiast, an endorser for broad public appeal, an objective resource just outside but intimately involved with the organ profession, and sometimes a 'devil's advocate' with a generalist viewpoint, also serving as a communicator and facilitator. By the way, none of us received any salary for our work.

JZ/ **What was the purpose of this committee?** JMB/ First we met to discuss strategy and create a list of potential builders. We sent out requests to a number of firms (American, French, Dutch, English, German and Danish) with either direct experience with concert hall organs, or with the imagined potential for this. Later we met to review the incoming proposals, of which there were about a dozen. These ranged in cost from $800,000 to over $2 million. At our first meeting, it was announced that $1 million had been received for the organ, which seemed like an unfortunate early limitation on a project we knew would need to cost more. The committee discussed the need for a modern mechanical-action organ that would produce a dynamic balance with the orchestra, but also requested proposals from builders of electric-action instruments.

JZ/ **Can you explain more about the dynamics?** JMB/ The aesthetics of organ tone go through cycles. In the U.S. the orchestrally-imitative concert organs of the 1920s and 1930s had been replaced in the post-war period by neo-classical instruments based on ideals from the 18th century. Today's audiences expect a much wider range of dynamics. Our artistic decisions were based on reasoned subjectivity. When we first met early in the 1990s, we hoped for a sound that most builders had not yet achieved. Idealistically, we wanted to coax our builder, whoever that might be, into something better than had previously been designed. The general attitude of the committee was to find a builder willing to be a bit adventuresome — going for a bigger, 'rounder' sound while still retaining classical nuances.

JZ/ **How did the committee gather information and ideas?** JMB/ Before selecting Manuel J. Rosales as the Tonal Designer, a sub-committee traveled around the U.S. evaluating several organs from different builders. Some of the LA Philharmonic people inspected other instruments in concert halls in Japan. Much later on, Manuel J.

Rosales and I were to do a follow-up there, but we were set to depart on September 11, 2001. Suffice it to say, international travel was restricted and the disruption of our schedule related to actual performance events in these halls thwarted that adventure.

JZ/ **What led the committee to choose Manuel J. Rosales and Glatter-Götz Orgelbau?** JMB/ We came to a conclusion regarding Rosales in less than a year after the first committee meeting. We chose him because of the impressive tonal effect of a recent, large instrument in Oakland, as well as various other projects, which showed him to be someone with great potential. That he was located in Los Angeles offered an additional efficiency which turned out to be valuable. He could interact with Gehry, answering questions and establishing a basic design related to the accommodation of a pipe organ in the proposed hall. Even with the finances of the entire Disney Hall project in flux, and the budget for the organ still uncertain, it seemed essential to engage Rosales to work with the architect so the structure of the building would accept an organ. After a period of years, when the project was revived, Rosales suggested a collaborator — a company already prepared to produce the complex components required — Glatter-Götz Orgelbau in Germany. The committee was impressed with the technical and engineering finesse of this company, so the notion of a joint project appeared totally reasonable. Their recently-completed joint project at the United Church of Christ in Claremont, pointed very much to the sound we hoped for in the Walt Disney Concert Hall. The collaborative proposal was reviewed and accepted by the WDCH and LA Philharmonic managers. Glatter-Götz would construct the instrument to a Rosales tonal recipe and a physical/visual design jointly created by Frank Gehry and Rosales. Gehry provided the vision, Glatter-Götz made that vision functional, and Rosales created the sound.

JZ/ **Were you involved with the organ installation?** JMB/ After the organ committee had done its work, I was retained to offer advice as needed. I was involved slightly in overseeing the design details of the console layout. Once some pipework was playing, I was invited out to inspect. Then, as the voicing progressed, I came out to listen and make comments. In the month prior to the AGO [American Guild of Organists] Convention 'preview' performance, I spent several days checking details, playing the organ, trying to get it to act up so that there would be no mechanical surprises at concert time. There were none, fortunately.

JZ/ **What are your feelings about this organ?** JMB/ The 'craziness' of the initial visual idea makes perfect sense in the context of the hall and the building. The organ is the 'Gehry emblem' in contrast to the auditorium's symmetrical layout, linked to the hall's overall asymmetrical contours and design. It is so much more impressive (and actually rather friendly and very much fun) in person than in its pictures — and the sound is everything we had hoped for!

ROSALES VOICING A FLUE PIPE

Manuel J. Rosales
Tonal Designer and Organ Voicer

At an early age, I became interested in classical music. My fascination with the pipe organ began when my father took me to see "Fantasia" on my 14th birthday. I was enthralled with this Walt Disney production and with the organ music of Bach. I was curious about the pipes and mechanisms that produced these wonderful sounds. Later, a summer job with the organ tuner of our church revealed some of the mysteries and made me feel that pipe organ building would become my life's work. So that's where it all began. Although I have a particular interest in the preservation and restoration of historic organs, there is nothing quite like the thrill of excitement I feel when designing a new instrument.

So, you can imagine how I reacted when I received a phone call in 1989 asking me if I would be interested in designing a pipe organ for the Walt Disney Concert Hall. The request was for a 'simple' organ, one that could play all of the organ literature, including all of the music for organ and orchestra, do all the things a concert hall organ is supposed to do — all for under $1 million! My excitement turned to consternation. Simple? It was almost impossible!

The earliest models showed the organ in the front and center of the concert hall. That pleased me, and I was intrigued. I wondered about the acoustics, and if people would even show up for organ concerts, but I wanted to be associated with this public project. Given the basic outline, and the budget of $1 million, the organ would have only 25 ranks at most, I thought. It would be small.

There were other fundamental factors to consider also. Working in Los Angeles, the costs would be enormous. It would take large sums of money just to build an earthquake-resistant structure for the organ. Many other organ builders refused to even consider the opportunity. What was really needed was about $3 million.

At first, I was one of about twenty bidders from around the world — then one of five, then one of three. Finally, in the summer of 1990, my company was given a contract to design the organ, not to build it. We were asked to work with the architect in defining the physical parameters of the organ — its space, and the electrical and mechanical considerations in fitting it into the interior of the hall. We were also responsible for the tonal design. This process, initially planned to require six months, continued for two and one-half years.

The architect, Frank Gehry, was unorthodox and innovative, acclaimed in other countries, but not in Los Angeles. He was known for his radical ideas, but also for his creative genius. At our first meeting, I took with me books showing various organ designs, thinking that would be the way to proceed. He was a bit brusque with me. He didn't want 'his' organ to look like what had already been done, so he wasn't interested in examining old pictures. His goal was to elevate the organ world to a new level, to build an organ so provocative, but so beautiful, that nobody would forget it. In retrospect, I am grateful to him for that, but at the time it was quite unsettling. Our collaboration proved to be both a stimulating challenge and a frustrating experience. He is a man of limitless imagination and creativity. Gehry knew nothing about organs, but he insisted that he would be in charge of the façade concept — the part seen by the viewing audience. Then he said to me, "It is your job to make sure everything I design will work!"

During this time, there were about 35 people in his office, most of them under 25. They were fresh with new ideas, totally open to anything Mr. Gehry wanted to try, and willing to transform his concepts into completed drawings and models. For over two years there was philosophical and sometimes heated debate between the two of us. I explored with him many designs, most of which could not be built for practical reasons. He had lots of ideas, sketched out in his characteristic squiggles and shapes, then transformed into scale models:

- Pipes wearing metal 'hats' and 'skirts' that angled outward
  (*The designer look*)
- Trumpet pipes hung from the ceiling
  (*How would I get to them for tuning?*)
- The organ partially hidden behind an enormous open basket design
  (*A statement for architects, but a horror for musicians*)
- The organ located behind giant wooden panels that would open up
  for a performance
  (*This would create a door-like barrier in front of the audience
  when not in use.*)
- A log jam of pipes (*Hmmm...that had possibilities*)

I was willing to consider that last one because it had the potential of looking like a real organ. Models were prepared in a scale of 1:24. I insisted that all pipes should be functional, not just for looks. We settled on two octaves of Violone in the front. Many organs have a façade, or screen, which hides most of the pipes. In this case, the largest wooden pipes became the façade. At first, these tall pipes were perfectly straight, but set at interesting angles. The model sat around for months, but Frank Gehry always wants to try something else, an improvement. One of his final ideas — an inspiration — was to make some of the pipes curved. Would they sound all right? More importantly, could they be built? I agreed — if the pipes were wood, and with only a mild curve. We made three test pipes, an 8-foot, a 16-foot, and a 32-foot Violone. They worked perfectly. The curve made no difference to the sound. Actually, it made the pipes more fun to voice, and the speech was better and faster. Then we added a starburst of trumpets for a center-piece — the now famous 'Trompeta de Los Angeles' — the brilliant Llamarada which reaches out and calls to you.

When the organ design was finished, the *Los Angeles Times* showed a picture of the table-top model in its primitive form and it received mixed reviews. I was satisfied with it, but what would other professionals think? I sent photos to my organ-building colleagues. Nobody replied at first. Then I began to get comments. "You're joking, aren't you?" "You're not really going to build this?" Well, we had worked on it for almost 3 1/2 years. I trusted Frank Gehry, and both of us were putting our careers on the line. But I needed a collaborator, a company that could actually build these pipes. Nobody I asked would commit to it. I was told: "It would ruin my firm…It will set back organ building one hundred years…Nobody will want to hear it." Thankfully, our detractors were proved wrong.

In the meantime, the whole concert hall project came to a standstill due to lack of funding. After the Northridge earthquake in 1994, there was no extra money available for the arts. There were more pressing needs. But the vision did not die. It was put on hold for another four years. Eventually, the resources were provided through massive fundraising efforts, and the Walt Disney Concert Hall project was revitalized. As early as 1995, the unfolding design for the organ had resolved itself into some definite decisions, but the overall tonal design was not clearly defined, nor the total budget. Eventually, the Toyota Motor Corporation generously provided the $3 million needed for completion as I had originally estimated.

My search for a collaborator to build this organ led me to Glatter-Götz Orgelbau, a German company with forward-looking ideas. At about this time, we were cooperating on a different project. My company, Rosales Organ Builders, provided the voicing, tonal design, and pipe scaling for a Glatter-Götz organ in Claremont, California. Both of our companies, as well as the church, were very pleased with the results. When I asked Caspar Glatter-Götz if he would join me in the Walt Disney Concert Hall project, he agreed without a second thought. He was willing, even eager, to seize this opportunity to build something different and innovative — a truly modern organ, utilizing technology his company already had. By the middle of 1998, the arrangements were concluded which allowed me to be the tonal director and Glatter-Götz to do the building and installation of this complicated instrument. The installation alone took about 12 months, beginning in October of 2002.

When the concert hall opened in the fall of 2003, members of the audience gasped with delight at its visual focus — the towering pipe organ façade occupying a central position at the rear of the stage. It was obvious that Frank Gehry had achieved his purpose. He had created a startling organ design to match the uniqueness of the building. But I still had a lot of work to do. The concert hall was completed and the organ in place, but it was silent. It would require at least a year of finishing before it could speak. Every one of the pipes had to be individually fine-tuned to a perfect pitch and tone, in relation to the acoustics of the hall. There were 6,134 pipes to adjust — most of them hidden behind that impressive façade.

"This pipe organ is a hand-built instrument of the highest quality which has taken over two years to construct and install, and another year for acclimatizing to the environment of the Walt Disney Concert Hall."

—Manuel J. Rosales

TUNING THE MAGNIFICENT
TROMPETA DE LOS ANGELES

The process of tuning and voicing took thousands of hours. It was fortunate that I lived only 15 minutes away. Mostly, I worked at night with my business associate of thirty years, Kevin Gilchrist. That late, the rehearsals and concerts were over and the hall was quiet. You can't have anyone else in the room making even a small noise. We took turns, one playing notes from the console while the other made adjustments in the voicing. We did not stop until we were satisfied with the results. The basic philosophy of our company is to achieve a tonal result which has grandeur, majesty and awe, balanced with clarity, delicacy and refinement — and that is what we have.

The organ's role in a concert hall goes beyond that of a church. There must be a high range of dynamics, as well as the deep bass tones that underpin the orchestral ensemble. We feel assured that the Walt Disney Concert Hall organ is a complete instrument on which can be played a wide array of organ literature. With a total of 72 registers on four manuals, this instrument has many unusual and interesting features and accessories.

This organ is an absolutely engrossing, incredibly complicated piece of machinery. In some ways it overwhelms you, and it stimulates your imagination. It is the culmination of so many years of work, and for me personally it is a grand success, a dream come true.

ROSALES CURVING A 32' BOMBARDE TONGUE

"If an organ is added to a concert hall, it is seldom in the most ideal position with a beautiful and still unique design. So, it was an advantage with the Walt Disney Concert Hall to have the architect include the pipe organ in his design. When the acoustical tests were done with one-tenth size models, the results were excellent. The complicated shapes of the walls and ceiling panels inside the hall, plus the almost sculptured surfaces of the facade, favor the organ. This instrument has many pipes with different tones, so the sound is scattered randomly throughout the concert hall which gives a pleasant acoustics."

—Yasuhisa Toyota, chief acoustician of the Walt Disney Concert Hall and Company Director, Nagata Acoustics

FULL MODEL OF HALL AND ORGAN

GILCHRIST TUNING THE PIPES

KEVIN GILCHRIST
Technical Director and Head Voicer
for Rosales Pipe Organ Services, Inc.

JZ/ **What was it like for you and Manuel J. Rosales to begin work on the Walt Disney Concert Hall pipe organ?** KG/ We needed a basic tonal concept, bare bones, but able to be enlarged if more funding became available. Because it was in Los Angeles, it was necessary to design a steel frame that would be earthquake resistant. We had already accomplished this for a church in Oakland, and we based our structural design on that. When we began our collaboration with Glatter-Götz Orgelbau in Germany, I turned our design over to Heinz Kremnitzer, their chief engineer, and I began work on pipe scaling.

JZ/ **Could you explain the term 'scaling'?** KG/ Scaling is determining the diameter of each pipe relative to its length, and matching these proportions to the size and acoustics of the room. We also consider factors such as materials, thickness, shapes, and styles.

JZ/ **How do you match the size of a pipe to the acoustics of a hall?** KG/ The Disney Hall is the largest space we have ever worked in, so we looked at charts and graphs from past projects, our own and others, and we made estimations. You start with the Principals and make selections based upon the sound you desire. You have to go with your personal judgment and experience. You do a lot of listening and adjusting. Before computers, it was written down by hand. Now, I make a computer graph and make comparisons quickly. Figuring out the measurements for the Disney organ pipes took a year. We always want the 'Rosales' sound, so there must be a great deal of thought before we send out the pipe orders.

JZ/ **What was the biggest challenge?** KG/ The large wooden pipes in the Gehry façade were the most difficult. Some of them are high up on a ledge and had to fit beneath the shape of the ceiling. We simply made an educated guess on a few of the dimensions. This was an important consideration in determining whether or not the curved wooden pipes of the Gehry façade would sound right. Three sample pipes were constructed by Glatter-Götz for this purpose, curved to the Gehry measurements. Manuel J. Rosales traveled to the GG workshop where he voiced and tuned these pipes. They were a complete success.

JZ/ **How many different kinds of pipes are there?** KG/ Basically, two: flue pipes which are resonating tubes, and reed pipes which have an oscillating reed at the small end of the cone. Within those two categories, pipes are open, closed, stopped with a cap that has a small chimney, tapered or straight. Many are made of different materials which affect the tone. For example, tapered pipes made of a tin alloy do not sound the same as straight wooden pipes of the same approximate dimensions.

JZ/ **Once you had the final specifications, where were all these pipes made?** KG/ All the wooden pipes were made in the Glatter-Götz workshop. The metal flues were made in Portugal, the reeds in Germany, and the pipes for the Llamada (the rooftop trumpet pipes) in England. All of them were assembled in the Glatter-Götz workshop. Manuel J. Rosales traveled there several times to assist with the pre-voicing.

JZ/ **Then everything was shipped from Germany to Los Angeles. How did that go?** KG/ Fortunately, it went well. All of the components were packed into six huge sea containers. I remember watching the movie, The Perfect Storm, which came out around that time. I could just envision what would happen to our shipment if it passed through that kind of hurricane with 100-foot waves. I thought to myself, "Well, there goes the Disney Hall organ!"

JZ/ **So, everything arrived intact and ready for installation. What about the voicing?** KG/ The team from Glatter-Götz efficiently installed the framing, casework, all the pipes, both consoles, and the three blowers. Then they checked to be sure everything was working properly — including the pipes which then had to be taken out again and stored on site. That's because it was necessary for us to tune and voice every single pipe, and we basically work from front to back inside the case. Where possible, I laid them out on a table by ranks and tested each one. We would set the sample 'C' pipes first in the organ, then voice and tune the pipes in between. In the voicing process, I would first blow them by mouth and listen to the tone, and make some changes. Then, for fine adjustments, I would use the voicing machine — which is just a small organ that is set to the same pressure that a given set of pipes will need.

JZ/ **There are many factors to consider. This sounds like a complex process.** KG/ It is. A change in diameter for a given length changes the tone. Flue pipes are more predictable while reeds are more difficult to voice. String pipes (made to simulate the tone of a stringed instrument) tend to be narrow, and they have richer

ACCESS LADDER INSIDE THE ORGAN CASE

The Rosales shop in Los Angeles is replete with file drawers containing research and order sheets including the final specifications for all 6,134 pipes.

harmonics. They can take a week to adjust. Principals and flutes are much easier. Even after they are back in the organ case, pipes may sound different due to the acoustics of the room and the reflections of the sound.

JZ/ **What exactly can you do to make these adjustments?**   KG/ On flue pipes, the cut-up — the height of the upper lip compared to the width of the mouth — can be raised, resulting in fewer overtones. It is also possible to lower a cut-up by cutting the pipe apart and soldering it back together again, but this is something we want to avoid. Tiny grooves, nicks, can be cut in the languid. Sharp edges can be filed off, or languids raised or lowered. All of these, and more techniques, are used to produce a refined speech and tone. Reed pipes are more limited in the changes that can be made, mostly confined to changing the curve of the tongue, and making it louder or softer by changing the length of the resonator.

JZ/ **It sounds as though the parts of these pipes are defined by the human anatomy.**   KG/ That's true. Starting at the conical bottom of a flue pipe, we speak of the toe, the foot right above it, then the mouth, which is the opening, the upper and lower lips, and the body which comprises the rest of the pipe. Then there can be ears on either side of the mouth. On a reed pipe, there is also a boot just above the toe.

JZ/ **What kinds of tools do you use for this process?**   KG/ We have wood-working and metal-working tools. We use dividers (like a map reader's) for making exact measurements, and we have various kinds of cutting instruments and files.

JZ/ **So, after the initial tuning was done, outside the case, all the pipes had to be installed again.**   KG/ Yes, all of the pipes for each of the five divisions had to be placed in their cases in a particular order, so we could get to them for the final voicing adjustments before they were hidden by the pipes standing in front of them. Sometimes we had to use a 'cherry-picker' to reach the façade pipes.

JZ/ **I suppose the final voicing would need to be done by two people. Is that right?**   KG/ Yes, Manuel played notes and listened from the console, and then described what was wrong — mostly saying 'louder' or 'softer' while I made adjustments. Most of these distinctions were very subtle and we had to listen carefully with no other noise in the hall. We created the sound we felt was right, the finest voice for each pipe. It was hard work. I lost five pounds during the first month just from climbing around among all those organ pipes. This process required infinite patience, and thousands of hours. That is why Manuel and I worked for a year to voice the Walt Disney Concert Hall organ.

CASPAR von GLATTER-GÖTZ
Organ Builder and Founder of Glatter-Götz Orgelbau, Owingen, Germany

jz/ **What is the philosophy of Glatter-Götz Orgelbau?** cgg/ We specialize in building contemporary instruments which we believe should far outlast the people who have created them. Our team consists of idealists who regard their work as a cultural contribution. Based on this philosophy, we build organs — with delicate and magnificent sounds — for churches, concert halls and private homes, so that others may play especially beautiful music on them.

jz/ **Since you have a great interest in producing visually spectacular organs, you must have eagerly agreed to collaborate on the Walt Disney Concert hall project.** cgg/ Yes, I was very enthusiastic. In fact, I was shown this organ design when I visited the office of Frank Gehry in 1995. At that time, we were working with Manuel J. Rosales on a new church organ in Claremont, California. He did the tonal work and I liked the sound of what he produced; and, he appreciated the craftsmanship and aesthetics of Glatter-Götz Orgelbau, so it was a good collaboration. During this time, the Disney Hall building project was revived as well as the plans for the pipe organ. Manuel J. Rosales was looking for a builder at that time who could and would produce this large and extremely complicated organ. He asked me if my company would be interested in collaborating. Of course I agreed! The contract was signed directly between Glatter-Götz and the Walt Disney Concert Hall organization in 1999. It was a 4-year project. During that time we were working on other organs simultaneously because there was a delay in the construction of the hall.

jz/ **How did your company organize such a massive undertaking from so far away?** cgg/ First, the complete design of the organ was defined with CAD drawings, including the visual design of the

movable console, which was created by my associate, Heinz Kremnitzer. Then materials were ordered, depending on when they were needed. We worked according to a production and payment schedule observed by the general building manager for the whole concert hall. Progress reports and pictures of the produced parts had to be sent every month to the manager's office in Los Angeles. Because of the use of CAD and digital photography, we communicated with Gehry's office very well and clarified all details in close cooperation with his staff. By exchanging drawings and photos over the internet, both sides could see what the other party was thinking or planning. The complete coordination between all parties concerned in designing, building, time-schedule and installation was in the hands of GGO.

JZ/ **Apart from the visual aspects of the organ, there must have been many engineering consid-** erations. CGG/ The engineering aspect, under the guidance of Heinz Kremnitzer, was done in close cooperation with the Gehry office, since we had to consider many details like earthquake safety, steel alloy, fitting the instrument into the organ loft, wind chest layout, calculating the bracing of the façade pipes, and particularly the exact positions and length of each façade pipe. The placing of those pipes was carefully planned by Gehry and his team and had to be executed exactly according to the intention of his design.

JZ/ **What about materials, such as the wood and metal?** CGG/ The façade pipes, the 32' pipes on the side of the case, as well as the casework itself, were all made of Douglas fir. We bought it from a large importer in Amsterdam, but it came from the United States. We carefully selected only the finest grained wood. Smaller quantities of other kinds of wood (cherry for the main console, spruce and oak for the inside pipes) were bought from our suppliers in Austria. We do not make our own metal pipes. We go to professionals who specialize in that. Manuel J. Rosales determined the scales for each rank and we followed those specifications. The complete steel framing inside the organ was built by a company close by.

JZ/ **How did you select the particular shops to make the metal pipes?** CGG/ Manuel gave us the names of shops, based on his confidence that these pipemakers would make specific stops in an optimal way according to his requirements. Many pipes were made in Germany, others in Portugal and England, to utilize the quality of workmanship there. All wooden pipes were made in our shop.

JZ/ **In addition to the wooden pipes your company made, what else did you provide?** CGG/ We did everything else. We bought the equipment for the electric stop action, like draw-stop solenoids, slider solenoids, and all the electronic parts for the capture system and the switching components. We also bought the motors to activate the Swell shutters.

JZ/ **How did you assemble everything?** CGG/ After the parts were produced, we preassembled the various divisions in our shop. One part was the Console, Positive and Pedal, another part was the Swell division, which is the size of a small living room. On a separate spot we preassembled the Llamarada division. Our whole shop, first and second floor, was totally full with the preassembled organ.

JZ/ **So, after you determined that everything fit together and worked properly, then what?** CGG/ Well, we disassembled the organ and shipped off the wind system and steel framing for an early delivery because they had to be incorporated into the building at the proper time. A crew of three organ builders, under the guidance of Heinz Kremnitzer, went to Los Angeles for that part of the installation. Originally the team consisted of four, but U.S. immigration officials refused entry to one member of the team — without the slightest explanation. Unfortunately, he was also the strongest man on the team, so it became a harrowing task for the reduced crew to do the job. About four months later the rest of the organ was shipped. It was unloaded with the assistance of some local labor, and put together on site by Heinz Kremnitzer and five of our organbuilders. This crew had worked on the production of the organ in the shop, so it was easy for them to assemble the organ again. After the organ was physically set up, the crew was reduced to complete the remaining technical work. Then the tonal finishing of the façade pipes was done by Rosales, together with Stefan Stürzer from Glatter-Götz Orgelbau.

ORGAN CASE PARTS WAITING FOR VENEER   JOACHIM SEIFRIED, THE CASE MAKER   AMERICAN DOUGLAS FIR
IMPORTED THROUGH AMSTERDAM

"Every great organ is the result of extraordinary collaboration, even when the product of a single firm. This organ represents unusually integrated teamwork among the builders, working together with architect, management, consultant, and voicer. Most particularly, it demonstrates Glatter-Götz's commitment to a vision of 21st century organbuilding capable of looking beyond the horizon."

—Jonathan Ambrosino, "Walt Disney Concert Hall," The American Organist, April, 2004

GERHARD MÖHRLE MAKING THE ORGAN BENCH

JZ/ **How did you pack and ship these various-sized parts from Germany to the U.S.?** CGG/ Some parts (steel framing, case work, bellows, wind ducts, blowers) were put into metal sea containers with corrugated cardboard or plastic bubble wrap for protection, along with some wooden bracing. More delicate parts were protected inside wooden crates. Trackers were carefully wrapped in paper. All the wooden façade pipes were wrapped in several layers of plastic bubble material. Metal pipes up to 4' were put in sturdy cartons with excelsior around them. Tin pipes of 32' - 16' - and 8' -length were packed in crates with Styrofoam protection. Inside each pipe were Styrofoam braces to prevent the metal from going flat. Such pipes are made out of a soft alloy of tin and lead so when stored horizontally they may collapse and get out of round. You can imagine what a huge pile of material we had! There were six sea-containers (four 40' and two 20' sea containers) weighing a total of 44 metric tons. The longest pipe was 32' long and weighed 800 pounds! The loaded containers were trucked from our shop to the nearest railroad station, then sent to the harbor in Bremen in Northern Germany. From there, they were put onto a ship for the ocean voyage to California. It took four weeks from Bremen to Los Angeles, across the Atlantic and through the Panama Canal.

JZ/ **How did you keep everything organized?** CGG/ Each crate and box had written on the outside everything that was in it. All parts were marked and labeled so the organ builders could easily find what they needed during the assembly on site. All organ pipes, along with their component parts, were identified by numbers and locations. We also had a packing list for each sea container for U.S. customs inspection.

JZ/ **The cost for materials and shipping alone must have been staggering!** CGG/ Yes, to send one 40' sea-container from our shop in Owingen to Los Angeles was $4,330. This is just the freight cost

PEDAL TOE BOARDS

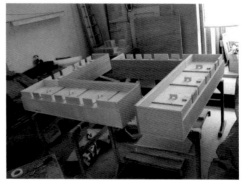

TOE BOARDS FOR HASKEL PIPES

"*Front and back were glued with many clamps to the curved sides. Because of the size of the large pipes and the fast drying of the glue, the work had to go fast. Up to eight people were needed to glue one pipe. Front and sides were glued together with a false tongue and groove. The exact size of the given scale was guaranteed and it gave extra strength at the joints. The wood was kiln-dried to 8.5% so it would not grow or shrink in the auditorium.*" —Caspar von Glatter-Götz

A FAÇADE PIPE UNDER CONSTRUCTION   CLAMPS HOLDING GLUED PIECES

"The curves for the wooden façade pipes were designed on CAD and plotted out on paper. A jig was made, and the contours of the right and left sides were drawn onto the wood and then cut with a band saw. Afterwards, the edges were carefully planed to a perfect curvature."
—Caspar von Glatter-Götz

without packing, loading and unloading. In summary: cost of materials was $945,964; cost of shipping was $32,141; the cost of insurance was $21,404. So that's a total of almost $1 million right there, not even counting labor costs for installation.

jz/ **And then there's the amount of time spent on this project. How did that break down?** cgg/ Design drawings — 1,050 hours. Construction — 25,501 hours. Installation in the U.S. — 5,747 hours. That's a total of 32,298 man-hours, or about 4,000 8-hour days for one person.

jz/ **This entire project has been an enormous achievement. Perhaps the creation of this unique instrument will inspire other cities to build pipe organs in concert halls. What do you see as the future trend?** cgg/ It looks hopeful. In the last few years, there has been a revitalized interest in

placing pipe organs of contemporary design in concert halls. I hope that future instruments will be as visually spectacular as this one at the Disney Hall, and that they will sound as beautiful. There are unlimited possibilities, and Glatter-Götz Orgelbau will continue to build innovative instruments of the highest quality.

GERHARD MÖHRLE RACKING THE PIPES
FOR THE LLAMARADA.

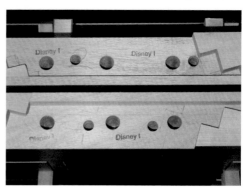

"Pipes have to be made very carefully and exactly. Larger pipes should be within 2 or 3 millimeters of accuracy, smaller ones within 1 millimeter. The very smallest must be within one-tenth of a millimeter."
—Caspar von Glatter-Götz

HEINZ KREMNITZER DRILLING THE
LLAMARADA CHEST TOP BOARD

MAIN CONSOLE UNDER CONSTRUCTION

TOE BOARDS READY TO RECEIVE FINISHED PIPES

SWELL FRONT WITH 'DISNEY 1' STAMP

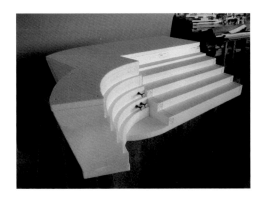

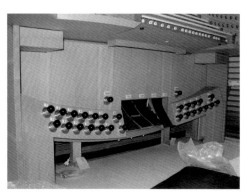

A STAGE CONSOLE STYROFOAM MODEL WAS USED
TO CHECK THE VISUAL AND FUNCTIONAL

THE CABINETRY IS COMPLETED, NO KNOBS IN PLACE,
BLUE TAPE FOR PROTECTION DURING SHIPPING

REAR VIEW SHOWING ELECTRICAL WORK

FRONT VIEW SHOWING PISTONS
AND EXPRESSION SHOES

WHILE THE CONCERT HALL APPEARED TO BE COMPLETE,
WORK CONTINUED INSIDE.

SHIPPED FROM BREMEN, GERMANY TO THE PORT OF LOS ANGELES,
COMPONENTS WERE THEN TRUCKED TO THE BUILDING SITE AND
CAREFULLY UNLOADED. AT TIMES, TRAFFIC AROUND THE MUSIC
CENTER COMPLEX HAD TO BE STOPPED.

ALL THE PARTS WERE STACKED ON THE STAGE
IN A PREDETERMINED ORDER. EACH CRATE HAD
BEEN LABELED. ALL THE ORGAN PIPES AND THEIR
COMPONENTS WERE IDENTIFIED BY NUMBERS
AND LOCATIONS.

EACH PIPE WAS GENTLY UNWRAPPED
AND INSPECTED.

THE STAGE CAT EXPLORED

THE STEEL FRAMING HAD BEEN ASSEMBLED EARLIER TO EXACT MEASURE-
MENTS, ACCURATE TO A MILLIMETER. AFTER IT WAS WELDED TOGETHER BY
U.S. TRADESPEOPLE, IT WAS COVERED WITH THREE COATS OF PAINT. THE
STEEL FRAMING WEIGHED ABOUT 30,000 POUNDS.

THE STEEL FRAMING WAS PUT IN PLACE SO THE FAÇADE PIPES COULD BE
SECURELY ANCHORED TO IT. FOR EARTHQUAKE SAFETY, THIS SUPPORTIVE
STRUCTURE HAD TO MEET THE STRICT REQUIREMENTS OF THE STATE OF
CALIFORNIA. THE STRUCTURAL CALCULATIONS WERE DONE IN GERMANY.

MASSIVE SECTIONS WERE HOISTED INTO PLACE AND FASTENED SECURELY.

SOME OF THE GERMAN WORKERS HAD TO BE PERSUADED TO USE HARNESSES.
THEY WERE NOT USED TO AMERICAN SAFETY REQUIREMENTS.

THE MAIN CONSOLE WAS LIFTED INTO PLACE BEFORE FAÇADE PIPES BLOCKED THE OPENING. THE CONSOLE WAS THEN CONNECTED MECHANICALLY TO THE VALVES THAT ALLOW AIR FROM THE WIND CHEST INTO THE PIPES.

EACH KEY IS CONNECTED TO A TRACKER, A THIN STRIP OF WOOD, USED FOR OPENING OR CLOSING THE VALVE. THERE IS ONE TRACKER AND ONE VALVE FOR EACH KEY ON THE KEYBOARD. WHEN A KNOB IS PULLED AND A STOP IS ON, AIR FLOWS INTO THE OPENED PIPES. TRACKERS CHANGE WITH THE HUMIDITY, SO THEY ARE SELF-ADJUSTING.

BEHIND THE SCENES THERE WERE PLENTY OF OTHER PARTS TO INSTALL
AS WELL AS THE ELCTRICAL COMPONENTS.

MANUEL, STEFAN AND VLADIMIR CHECKING THE CONNECTIONS

THE STAGE CONSOLE, ORIGINALLY BUILT AND TESTED IN GERMANY, WAS REASSEMBLED IN LOS ANGELES

THERE ARE 6,134 PIPES, RANGING IN SIZE FROM A TELEPHONE POLE
TO A DRINKING STRAW, ARRANGED IN 109 RANKS.

THE PIPES FOR THE LLAMADA WERE POSITIONED
HORIZONTALLY ON THE VERY TOP OF THE ORGAN CASE.

ENCLOSED DIVISIONS OF PIPES ARE INSTALLED
BEHIND SLATS THAT CAN BE OPENED OR CLOSED
TO ALLOW THE SOUND TO EMANATE OR BE MUTED.
THIS MECHANISM IS CONNECTED TO A PEDAL WHICH
THE ORGANIST CAN MANIPULATE. UNENCLOSED
DIVISIONS OF PIPES REMAIN AT A CERTAIN LEVEL
OF VOLUME WHICH CANNOT BE ADJUSTED.

SWELL SHADES OR LOUVERS ARE USED TO CONTROL
THE VOLUME. SOME LOUVERS ARE VERTICAL AND
OTHERS HORIZONTAL.

THE VOICE OF AN ORGAN REQUIRES A CONSTANT FLOW OF AIR.

SPECIAL DUCTS CARRY THE AIR FROM THE WINDCHEST TO THE PIPES.
THIS AIR IS KEPT UNDER PRESSURE WITH THE USE OF THREE BLOWERS
SET AT DIFFERENT LEVELS: LOW - 6 1/2 COLUMN INCHES, MEDIUM - 7
COLUMN INCHES, AND HIGH - 17 1/2 COLUMN INCHES.

THE HIGHER PRESSURES ARE FOR THE LARGER PIPES. THERE IS ALSO AN
OIL REGULATOR FOR EACH BLOWER.

THE ORGANIST CAN CHOOSE FROM AN
ARRAY OF KNOBS, KEYS AND PISTONS.

THE MAIN CONSOLE

CASPAR VON GLATTER-GÖTZ, FRANK GEHRY AND YASUHISA TOYOTA GAZING
OUT ON THE CONCERT HALL FOLLOWING THE INAUGURAL PERFORMANCE.

*"Not a single façade pipe position or length is accidental.
One can say it is a carefully planned chaos!"*
—Caspar von Glatter-Götz

"With pipes bursting from the floor and the surrounding surfaces of the organ case,
these functioning façade pipes provide a visual bouquet as well as the tonal foundation
of the sound of the organ. Inside and behind this playing façade of wood pipes, there
are over 6,000 other pipes, made of metal alloys, which provide a vast tonal array
of sound available through the four keyboards and the pedals." —MANUEL J. ROSALES

JOANNE PEARCE MARTIN
Principal Keyboardist, Los Angeles Philharmonic

JZ/ **When did you first play the Walt Disney Concert Hall pipe organ?** JPM/ In the early summer of 2004, as the orchestra's keyboardist, I had the privilege and pleasure of playing the last movement of the Saint-Saëns Organ Symphony with the Philharmonic in a much-anticipated rehearsal. This was to be the first time any of the L.A. Phil people (including Esa-Pekka Salonen) would hear the instrument we had been admiring visually for months. I had worked closely with Manuel J. Rosales the previous week, getting to know the instrument a bit, and setting up the appropriate registrations. Esa-Pekka Salonen asked an assistant to conduct so that he could go out into the hall and hear the blend of the organ and orchestra from an audience standpoint. The first run-through was a real thrill for me. I actually had tears of joy and excitement in my eyes as I played this powerful music on this magnificent instrument with our fabulous orchestra in our incredible new home. It was overwhelming. After the last triumphant chord faded away, Salonen called out from the audience: "We need to do it again — we can't hear the organ!" Of course, it was a joke, and everybody burst out laughing. All of us were awed by the beauty and power of the organ. We did it again, however, just to give it a second listen. What a great day. I'll never forget it.

JZ/ **A couple of months later, you heard the organ played at the convention of the American Guild of Organists. This time, it was Cherry Rhodes playing, and you were a member of the orchestra. What was that like?** JPM/ I don't think I've ever felt such a collective sense of anticipation as I did that day from the audience of organists and organ-lovers at Disney Hall. This was the first audience to experience 'live in concert' the wonderful new instrument which had already created

JOANNE PEARCE MARTIN SITTING AT THE STAGE CONSOLE

such a stir solely with its looks. Our conductor for that concert, Alexander Mickelthwate, was also very caught up in the moment — it was obvious. He had of course furiously studied this newly-commissioned work, the *Concierto de Los Angeles*, and he was brilliant in shaping the orchestra to balance and complement the organ for this performance. Cherry Rhodes played magnificently, as always. I think the fact that we were performing a brand new work that was 'hot off the press' even added an extra layer of excitement to the experience, both for the performers and the audience.

JZ/ **Under what other circumstances have you played the organ at the Walt Disney Concert Hall?** JPM/ I performed a short, private program last season for a select group of LA Phil donors who dined afterwards at four tables actually set up onstage! I've also played the instrument quite a few times within the orchestral setting. Several premieres of new works we have played in the last two seasons have incorporated the use of the organ. In these circumstances, I prefer to play from the remote console placed in my normal keyboard position on stage right. This affords me the ability to hear the balance between the organ and orchestra, and it also gives me a clear view of the conductor without using the video camera and monitor set-up (which, by the way, works beautifully for an organist sitting at the main console — up among the façade pipes).

Then there were five performances of a wonderful show, celebrating the organ, designed for kids. This show included actors and dancers, the full orchestra, and myself — playing both the main and remote consoles. We performed Bach, Lou Harrison, and a medley of popular tunes which showed the versatility of the instrument and the different contexts in which we have all heard organ music in our lives — at the ball park, the carnival, in church, etc. One segment of the show featured me playing only the pedals while a dancer mimicked my movements by dancing on a large keyboard mat, as in the movie *Big*. The kids were delighted.

DR. ROBERT TALL
Coordinator for 2004 AGO Convention

As coordinator for the 2004 National Convention of the American Guild of Organists, Dr. Robert Tall was extremely interested in obtaining permission to use the new Walt Disney Concert Hall as a major venue. The magnificent organ, with its unconventional façade of enormous wooden pipes, was scheduled to be completed that summer. What a bonus it would be for this gathering of organists from around the country to hear a spectacular, new instrument! So he met with the administrators of the Los Angeles Philharmonic and persuaded them that the AGO Convention in July of 2004 would provide a perfect opportunity for a private 'rehearsal' for the new organ before its public debut in September. The evaluating comments of over 2,000 organists would furnish useful responses, free from media review. It would also prepare the conductor and orchestra for the experience of performing with this innovative pipe organ.

The Los Angeles Philharmonic agreed, and Robert Tall began spending quite a bit of time at the Walt Disney Concert Hall in preparation. This was during the summer of 2003, a full year before the convention. Manuel J. Rosales, the Tonal Designer and Finisher, invited him to check on the progress of the organ and to play from the main console. Later on, when most of the voicing had been done, pre-recorded improvisations were played back through the organ system. This allowed Dr. Tall and others to walk around the hall and listen to the sound from various locations.

The AGO rented the hall for July 8, 2004. Three exceptional organists played at the Convention, with members of the Los Angeles Philharmonic, and Alexander Mickelthwate conducting. Opening the program was Cherry Rhodes, internationally-acclaimed recitalist and Professor of Organ at the University of Southern California. She performed the *Concierto de Los Angeles* by James Hopkins, the world premiere of a masterful work for organ and orchestra commissioned by the AGO for this occasion. Following that was Joseph Adam, Principal Organist at St. James Cathedral in Seattle, Washington, and faculty member at the University of Puget Sound, who played three pieces. First, he performed the stirring *Fantasia über B-A-C-H* composed by Max Reger. This was followed by *Naïades* by Louis Vierne, a more delicate piece; then, *Hommage à Igor Stravinsky* by Naji Hakim, a work imbued with delightful rhythms and harmonies. The program ended with Robert Parris, University Organist and Professor of Music at Mercer University, Georgia. Dr. Parris played *Concerto No. I in C Major* by Leo Sowerby. This imposing work was originally written for E. Power Biggs, and Dr. Parris is the only person still living to have publicly performed it with an orchestra.

ROBERT TALL PLAYS, AND MANUEL J. ROSALES PULLS OUT THE KNOBS,
WHILE TESTING REED STOPS FROM THE MAIN CONSOLE.

"This is a beautiful instrument. It provides an extra allure to the concert hall. I expected Frank Gehry to come up with a unique design for the façade, and he certainly did. It is like no other, absolutely resplendent! This organ has a wonderful tonal range. We wanted a flexible instrument that could be used for all styles of music, from Baroque to contemporary music, solo or with orchestra. We were all very thrilled with the way it turned out. I hope it will be used frequently."

—ERNEST FLEISCHMANN, CLASSICALLY-TRAINED IMPRESARIO AND FORMER EXECUTIVE VICE PRESIDENT AND MANAGING DIRECTOR OF THE LOS ANGELES PHILHARMONIC AND THE HOLLYWOOD BOWL FOR 30 YEARS

CHERRY RHODES, ALEXANDER MICKELTHWATE, AND MEMBERS OF THE LOS ANGELES PHILHARMONIC ORCHESTRA, RECEIVING ACCOLADES FROM AN ENTHUSIASTIC
AUDIENCE OF OVER 2,000 ORGANISTS AFTER THE PERFORMANCE OF THE HOPKINS *CONCIERTO DE LOS ANGELES* AT THE AGO CONVENTION, JULY 8, 2004

CHERRY RHODES
Los Angeles Organist

JZ/ **It must have been especially satisfying for you to be involved in the process of selecting the designer and builder of this organ and then to perform on the resulting product.** CR/ It certainly was. What a fantastic experience it has been. It was very interesting and educational serving on the selection committee which considered many applicants before choosing Manuel J. Rosales, LA's widely-esteemed organ builder and the tonal designer of the organ, who in turn chose Orgelbau Glatter-Götz from Germany to build it according to his specifications. Then, to experience making music on this amazing instrument has been so exhilarating.

JZ/ **Do you think Dr. Hopkins' work showcases the broad variety of organ tone colors available on this instrument?** CR/ Absolutely — to the fullest. This organ has a lot of inner beauty and variety, and his concerto brings it out. It is written so that the organ interweaves with the orchestra. There are times when you almost wonder — was that the organ, or an orchestral instrument? The Spanish trumpets are used in a dialogue with the orchestra. Jim Hopkins achieves marvelous effects with organ and percussion. There are impressionistic and jazzy parts. He provides a colorful palette of sound. The opening and closing are almost ethereal — mysterioso!

JZ/ **When his score was given to you, were all the registrations indicated, or could you choose your own?** CR/ Jim was specific in some places, but left the registrations up to the performer in others. For example, there was one section where he indicated that each short phrase should have a different sound. So at times I would incorporate a reed, mutations, flutes, or a principal that would interweave with the solo instruments of the orchestra. In order to decide what to use, I would ask myself: What instrument is playing? What would be a nice contrast to it, or what would be in the same family, but have a different shading? I really enjoy this kind of detective work. Jim finished writing the concerto before he had heard the completed organ, so he left it to me to work out the color concepts. It was very exciting for both of us to hear the concerto come together for the first time in rehearsal.

JZ/ **In terms of the mechanics and electronics of the system, is this organ easy to use?** CR/ Oh, yes. Fabulous! There is a 'Next' button, a sequencer that allows the organist to progress through the succession of registrations from the beginning to the end of the piece. One can concentrate so much better on the music instead of wondering which button to push. Also, the sequencer greatly expands the palette of the instrument by giving easy access to the array of colors. With it, I was able to customize crescendos from pianissimo to fortissimo. Of course, this was a new organ, so there were a few mechanical adjustments to be made. By the time the audience heard it, everything was working very well.

JZ/ **What is it like to play from the upper console, right in the midst of the façade pipes?** CR/ It's an experience-and-a-half! Of course it depends upon what you are playing, and how much organ you are using. When you play the enchamade or horizontal trumpets, it is absolutely deafening. When you play quieter passages, it is delightful. The action is great on the upper console. When you depress the key, the sound is quite immediate.

JZ/ **How does that compare to playing on stage with the other musicians?** CR/ When playing the remote console on stage, there is a slight delay because the pipes are at a distance from the organist. You must anticipate the sound of the orchestra in order to be with it. That becomes a part of the timing, so you must listen acutely every moment. I prefer to be on stage with the other musicians because I want to be able to breathe together and feel the synergy. In my opinion, this cannot happen if the organist is far away from the other musicians, looking at the conductor on a little screen. It is very important to me to feel like we are all one entity breathing life into the music. On this occasion, everything was new, exciting, and unknown! All of us were getting used to hearing this big pipe organ, and hearing each other.

JZ/ **I suppose the score would dictate when the orchestra would be dominant, and when the organ?** CR/ Yes, that's true, but also much of that is up to the conductor and the musicians. When using more transparent colors, the orchestra has to adjust to the organ dynamics. There are certain sounds and dynamics that cannot be changed on the organ. In other instances, adjustments on both sides can be made if the passage needs to be louder or softer.

JZ/ **How did you prepare for this performance?** CR/ First I studied the full score of the concerto. I wanted to give it the maximum variety of color. The composer was specific in some places. In the unmarked sections, imagination was my guide.

I marked in the score where I wanted interpretive nuances. Then I requested a private rehearsal with the conductor, Alexander Mickelthwate, before the first orchestra rehearsal so we could talk about the work and what we wanted to do with it musically. Sometimes, organists must educate conductors about the organ, because it is so unlike any instrument they are used to conducting; but, Alexander Mickelthwate plays the organ himself, so it was easier to work with him. He is young and open, and we had a creative and congenial collaboration. We were on the same wavelength. It was an unusual situation: we were both making our debuts at the Walt Disney Concert Hall; and, this commissioned work was making its debut also!

JZ/ **Since this was a world premiere, and there were no recordings to listen to, how did you put this all together?** CR/ Because rehearsal time is always at a minimum in a concert hall, I was given a digital orchestration of the work on CD which James Hopkins and Dr. Robert Tall (the AGO Convention Coordinator) kindly made for practice purposes. This was painstakingly put together by recording the parts of each individual instrument, utilizing a computer software program and a keyboard. This allowed me to practice at home in preparation for playing with orchestra. Jim also made a piano reduction of the orchestral score and brought it to my house so we could rehearse it together. He played the orchestra parts on the piano, and I played the organ part, in my living room. Since the Disney organ was not quite fin-

ished, I practiced nearby at the Cathedral of Our Lady of the Angels, which also has an instrument of four manuals. I went through the motions to get the feel of the work on a large instrument. Unlike other instruments, with the organ you need to practice the mechanics and choreography of manual and piston changes — especially on a large organ. It's a kinesthetic 'workout.'

JZ/ **What factors must you consider when playing with an orchestra?** CR/ Every conductor is different and the orchestra reflects this. You must see immediately how the musicians react to that particular person's beat. When playing from the stage console, the organist is removed from the organ pipes, and there is a slight delay from the time the fingers touch the keys to when the sound is actually heard. The members of the orchestra, on the other hand, have direct contact with their instruments. The woodwinds and brass have an immediate attack, so the organist must come in sooner to be with them. The strings ease into their parts, so the organ can come in a bit later. When there is full orchestra, I come in with the woodwinds, percussion, and brass players. So it is important to really know the score and the orchestration: to know when to 'dive in' or not, and how to continue according to the variances in orchestration and textures.

JZ/ **When this work was commissioned by the AGO, it was to be a challenging work, but accessible to other organists. They wanted a piece that could be played again and again by others,** not music that would be performed once and then sit on the shelf. Do you feel that it meets these criteria? CR/ Yes, I think it is an accessible work that is very beautiful, poetic, dramatic, intriguing, and challenging. I hope it will be played for many years to come. Technically, perhaps, it is not that difficult. However, throughout the piece there are some rhythmical and lyrical sections that have tricky timings while weaving in and out of the orchestra. They were difficult to play, but oh, so much fun! Selecting registrations that were interesting and creative was a mental challenge. This is not a piece for an inexperienced organist. It would need someone advanced to realize the full potential of the music. If it were played on a more modest instrument than that of Walt Disney Concert Hall, it could still be effective. It might not have all the variety of color, but one would adjust the concept to fit a more limited instrument, and I think it would be very successful.

JZ/ **How would you describe the style of this organ?** CR/ It's definitely oriented toward a symphonic style of instrument. However, literature from all periods can be played successfully on it. It works well both as a solo instrument and also as an instrument with orchestra.

JZ/ **On what other occasions have you played the Walt Disney Concert Hall pipe organ?** CR/ In October, 2004, I participated in the Grand Avenue Festival, which was geared towards children. Manuel J. Rosales and I demonstrated the organ for ten minutes. Then I played a short program.

The kids were some of the most responsive listeners I have ever encountered. They were extremely quiet while I played, and when the music ended they were yelling and stomping as if it were a rock concert.

JZ/ **The Los Angeles Times described you as "fearless...as [you] traversed the varied moods...with expert proficiency..." when you played Joseph Jongen's** *Symphonie Concertante for Organ and Orchestra*, **Opus 81. This was in April, 2005, with the Los Angeles Philharmonic. Can you tell me about those three performances?** CR/ Ever since I was a teenager, I adored this fantastic work and wondered if I would ever have the opportunity to play it. It was literally a childhood dream come true to play the Jongen on such a magnificent organ in a most extraordinary hall, with one of the greatest orchestras in the world — truly an incredible experience! This 35-minute monumental work, written in 1926, is very different from the Hopkins concerto. I used totally different combinations of sounds, and as a result I had the opportunity to explore other wonderful aspects of the instrument. Edo de Waart was the guest conductor. He is a seasoned conductor and had already recorded this work. We both had definite musical ideas. The more we collaborated and rehearsed, the closer we were to becoming a musical team. By the first concert, we were very much in sync. To have been able to perform this work three times was a bit of heaven.

JZ/ **How does this instrument compare to other pipe organs you have played?** CR/ I do not think that this organ can be compared with any other. This is a great organ in a great space. I am unable to separate them. For me, the organ and hall are one — not "there's the organ, and there's the hall," so to speak. Visually, they meld together beautifully. There is nothing like it in the world — utterly stunning and forward-looking! It sounds fabulous, and it has been magnificently constructed. For the organ to flourish and evolve, we have to breathe new compositions into its bellows and pipes. That's one of the reasons why the Hopkins work is so exciting and important. It creates new life for the instrument so that the organ adventure can continue through this century and beyond.

CHERRY RHODES PLAYS AT THE GRAND AVENUE FESTIVAL OCTOBER 18, 2004

DR. JAMES F. HOPKINS
Los Angeles Composer and Organist

The James Hopkins organ concerto, commissioned by the American Guild of Organists for its 2004 National Convention, was premiered in the Walt Disney Concert Hall by members of the Los Angeles Philharmonic Orchestra with organist Cherry Rhodes. A review written by Timothy Howard in *The American Organist* described it in these words: *"James Hopkins' Concierto de Los Angeles was the best-integrated organ concerto I have heard, weaving individual voices of the organ in and out of complementary instruments in the orchestra… I wanted to hear the piece again as soon as it died away."*

JZ/ **What do you consider the most dramatic feature of this Walt Disney Concert Hall pipe organ?** JH/ Probably its physical appearance — those towering, curved wooden pipes that are the visual centerpiece of the hall. As one reviewer commented, it is the best-known organ façade in the world! Besides that, it was an engineering feat to construct and install! Because the 32' Violonbasse and 32' Contrebasson emanate from those visually dramatic façade pipes, I included a six-measure solo specifically for the pedals, using the Violonbasse. Some of the orchestral players couldn't believe how low it sounded.

JZ/ **Where do you begin in composing a commissioned work for such a complex instrument?** JH/ The commission was finalized in February 2001, but there was no Disney Hall organ at that point. I had obtained a stop list from Manuel J. Rosales a bit earlier and had several discussions with him regarding the proposed instrument. However, there were requirements in the commission that provided some framework for the piece. The length was to be 15-20 minutes, and a completed copy of the full score was due by July of 2003. Dr. Robert Tall, the convention coordinator, also made it clear that he wanted this work to be accessible to other concert organists, both in musical style and in technical demands. He wanted it to have a life of its own after the AGO Convention — not too avant garde or too demanding on the listener. He wanted melodies that people could enjoy, and he wanted lots of contrast to show off the instrument, not just a single developmental concept. So I began with the basic melodic material and then manipulated it into two major sections.

JZ/ **Could you describe it for us?** JH/ The first part, *Vision escondida (hidden vision)* has a quiet, ethereal introduction with small glittery sounds and no sense of established beat. The main theme is presented in two- or three-note fragments by the orchestral brass, followed by the entire theme in the solo organ. Subsequent thematic statements are embellished by increasingly elaborate ornamentation. This develops into a display of the organ's many tonal colors, leading to a series of dramatic fanfares and a short organ flourish in the cadenza. In the second part, *Vision revelada (revealed vision)* the main theme is transformed into an accompanied fugue. The mood changes to jazz-derived harmonies, dance-like rhythms and insinuating contours, building to a dramatic climax. Then the piece returns to the intimate and tranquil atmosphere of the opening.

JZ/ **Is it difficult to compose for an organ you haven't actually heard?** JH/ Not really. You know the generic sounds, and there are predictable families of pipes. Although, I must say that when I first heard the organ, it was not as loud and dramatic as I had expected. Another important influence came from an organ concerto I had heard some years earlier. I ended up truly hating it, partly because so much of the piece was consumed with both organist and orchestra playing the same material simultaneously. Also, one reviewer commented on the grand *fff* ending bringing the audience to its feet in the 'mandatory standing ovation.' That did not please me. The honor of audience approval should not come just because the piece ends with a loud flourish. As a result of my intense dislike for that other concerto, I vowed to avoid organ/orchestra doubling as

much as practical, and decided to have my concerto end extremely quietly.

JZ/ **But I remember, because I was there, that the audience rose to its feet in a spontaneous standing ovation — and applauded for over two minutes! It was so well-deserved — for you, for the organ, and for the organist.** JH/ Yes, that was certainly gratifying. It was a pleasure to write this commissioned piece, and to work with Cherry Rhodes as well as members of the Los Angeles Philharmonic.

JZ/ **What are the similarities and differences between composing an organ concerto and composing other works?** JH/ Among the obvious similarities is of course the desire to write music that will appeal to both performer and listener. Beyond that, the specifics of the composition or the performance medium play a very important role. One of my earliest concerns had to do with the fact that a large organ can function as a grand orchestra in many ways: variety of color, dynamic range, etc. Since many of the organ's colors are very similar to those of the orchestra, I wanted to make sure that the organ was heard separately when I wanted it to, and, conversely, that it blend in perfectly within the orchestral tone at other points.

JZ/ **How does a composer balance the sound of an organ with orchestral instruments? For instance, do you try to avoid direct comparison between a 'real' trumpet and the trumpet stop on the organ?** JH/ At certain points I used tone qualities unique to the organ. At others, I purposely asked for organ voices which are imitative of orchestral instruments. For example, although the instrumentation only requires two flutes, there is an exposed passage which features 3 or 4 flutes. Of course, some of these are from the organ. During the passage which leads to the second large section of the piece, there are a number of very ominous brass fanfares. Here, the orchestral brass (3 trumpets, 4 horns, 3 trombones and tuba) were mixed with many of the organ reeds. The result was the impression of an enormous brass section.

JZ/ **How do you, as an individual, compose organ music?** JH/ I begin by spending as much time as necessary to have a good mental picture of how the piece will 'look.' What is the overall profile? Dynamics? Texture? Range? How will the piece begin and end? Will it be sectional, seamless, or both? To what extent is it desirable for the listener to be aware of my methods of musical integration? It is only after a great deal of thought on these matters that I get down to the 'note' level. At this point, I now consider pitch material, both melodic and harmonic. Once I have decided on the basic material, I spend a great deal of time working and reworking. This includes all the standard manipulations that are the regular artistic tools of the composer: augmentation/diminution, inversion, interval expansion/contraction, octave displacement, changes in rhythm, etc. In this piece, the increasingly elaborate ornamentation was calculated from the beginning. I wanted to make sure the basic motive was established in the listeners'

minds, then followed by fancier, more elaborate versions. Since I consciously try to write very idiomatic music for every instrument or voice, I consider what are the inherent limitations of the particular medium. This is where a thorough understanding of the technical properties of the instrument and the performer come into play.

JZ/ **When you wrote this organ concerto did you know who the organist would be?** JH/ Not really, but Cherry Rhodes would have been my first choice. There is one passage of about 3 minutes in length in which I encourage the organist to use a huge variety of colors. Concertos are typically vehicles for the display of the featured soloist, so there is often a large passage with lots and lots of notes, designed to let the performer show off. I have been familiar with Cherry Rhodes' playing for about 30 years. She is incredibly talented, so this 'passage work' was appropriate for both her and the Disney Hall organ. Her registrations are masterful. She uses subtle nuances and more combinations than most performers. (Once, when she played in Paris, she followed an organist who used only 6 combination pistons. Cherry used 124.) Cherry has played a number of my other works, including two pieces commissioned for her, so she already knew my style of writing. There was a temptation to include even more difficult passages, but I kept in mind the admonition of Robert Tall to keep this work accessible to any very good organ recitalist.

JZ/ **How did the rehearsals go for this organ premiere?** JH/ The orchestra parts were delivered in April of 2004. The first rehearsal took place on July 6th, two days before the performance. My attendance at the rehearsals was primarily to ensure that the players and the conductor played exactly what was on the page. The score is carefully marked and edited — it needs very little 'interpretation.' Of course, there were matters of balance. In spite of the numerous favorable comments on the hall's acoustics, there are problems. The organ is considerably quieter when heard from the first 15-20 rows than it is from seats above stage level. Some of the orchestra players had problems in hearing the organ because it is designed to project outward, not downward. I sat about halfway back in the auditorium, so I had to run down to the stage to talk with the conductor. The players often couldn't hear the balance between the organ and their instruments, so they had to be told. The conductor, Alexander Mickelthwate, came fully prepared. He had almost no questions about the score and had clearly done meticulous preparation. The only recurring problem during the rehearsals (and the performance) was that the string players in general did not believe that *ppp* means very quiet. They seemed to think that lots of 16th notes must surely be important, and therefore must be played loudly for the audience to hear the detail. That was not my intent.

JZ/ **So, if your *Concierto de Los Angeles* is to have a continuing life, it must have been published.** JH/ Yes, it is available from Morningstar Organ Music in St. Louis, Missouri. The orchestral score and individual parts may be rented. It is appropriate for any large organ with at least three manuals, and with a generous combination action memory. The solo organ part, with a piano reduction of the orchestral score for rehearsal only, may be purchased.

JZ/ **If you were to compose another work for this organ, would you emphasize different tonal features?** JH/ If it were for solo organ, I would probably write more sections that are rather loud. Many casual listeners assume that because an organ can play extremely loudly, that it should, so they might expect that. Also, I might not require so many registration changes. One of the points of this commission was to show off the new organ, so I used as many different colors as were reasonable.

"It is a richly textured score, a beautiful exploration of instrumental timbres…organic and orchestral."
—MICHAEL BARONE, HOST OF PUBLIC RADIO SHOW PIPEDREAMS,
IN REFERENCE TO THE JAMES HOPKINS CONCIERTO DE LOS ANGELES

PHILIP SMITH AT THE STAGE CONSOLE

PHILIP ALLEN SMITH
Organ Conservator

Philip Smith is ecstatic about being the Conservator of the Walt Disney Concert Hall organ. He works with the Los Angeles Philharmonic and the Master Chorale. He meets with all of the organists who are preparing for a performance, showing them the instrument and answering questions. Then he plays for various groups: volunteers, patrons, children and adults. "I find the right repertoire for here," he says, "but Bach's *Toccata and Fugue in D Minor* is still the all-time favorite." Only once, just for fun, did he actually use every stop on the organ at the same time — using couplers.

As part of his duties, he also arranges for maintenance and tuning. "The concert hall is kept at a fairly constant temperature, 68-72 degrees, and humidity of 35-40%," he explained. Even so, changes in the environment affect the pitch, and occasionally something needs to be repaired or adjusted. "At the beginning, a few of the pull stops began to come out all by themselves," he said, "and sometimes the electronic parts need a bit of tweaking." The most unusual aspect of his job is to water the 'little birds' — the Pajaritos. These two tiny pipes are set upside down in water. When they are played they whirl around, and the air bubbles out of them in a warbling high-pitched bird call.

"The pipe organ is the original synthesizer — and has been for the last 1,000 years," Phil enthused while demonstrating the organ. When he played an ascending scale on the foot pedals, the notes emanated from alternate sides of the façade because the pipes are set in geometric opposition. It's like hearing it in stereo. The author was also surprised by a 'poof' of air against her ankle.

It came from the base of one of those giant wooden façade pipes — like the breath of a gentle dragon.

However, hearing the louder reed stops from the upper console can be unbearable at full volume. The Positive is right in your face, the Swell sounds from way up high, and the bassoons are directly above you. Some of the visiting organists have insisted on ear plugs while practicing. Some of the nearer orchestra members use ear plugs, also. Although audience seats are provided in this area behind the stage, it would be wise to sit to the extreme right or left of the instrument for an organ concert — the decibels are so high.

Phil explained that the organ is designed for concert use, not to imitate the sounds of other instruments, but to complement them. It can overpower the orchestra, or it can be overpowered. Describing the various divisions of this unique instrument, the Conservator started at the top, **Manual IV**, the *Llamarada*. It includes an array of pipes which are positioned horizontally on the very top of the organ case — the *Llamada*, which has the round sound of an English trumpet. The *Campanitas* is a specialized stop with two sets of bells that sound like the traditional *Zimberlstern*.

In **Manual III**, the Swell division, there are many French-sounding stops, from the loud *Bombarde* and *Trompette* to the softest *Celeste* and *Voix Angelique*. **Manual II**, the Great, has a whole set of bassoons (4-, 8-, 16- and 32-foot). The long, thin pipes in the case provide the deepest sound. It is so low, you can count the cycles. The longer, fatter pipes are the *Violonbasse* and have a softer, string sound. The reed stops provide a wonderful chorus. The Great manual is the only one that is unenclosed, meaning that the volume cannot be controlled by opening and closing the louvered shutters. An increase in volume is achieved by adding more stops to make a fuller sound. One hears another set of strings, horns, trombones, trumpets, tympani, and basses, as new pistons are touched. "It's like starting with a string quartet and adding more musicians." is Phil's analogy.

The bottom keyboard, **Manual I**, the Positive, includes stops that are more German, but it also has a beautiful *Cor anglais* (English horn). The Pedal division adds the powerful bass notes that provide a strong foundation. Some of these pedal tones come from the wooden pipes of the organ façade, others from pipes hidden behind it. Finally, there is the wonderful *Trompeta de Los Angeles* — the 8' trumpet pipes positioned horizontally above the organ console. The bright sounds of this array can be accessed from every manual.

As with any modern organ, this one has many electronic controls including combinations, couplers and pistons that allow the organist 300 memory levels for preset registrations. The upper or main console includes a small closed-circuit TV screen so that the organist can see the conductor on stage. The remote console is movable and can be plugged in at four different locations on the stage. Both consoles are equipped with electric action and allow digital recording for playback. "This is helpful for visiting organists," Phil explained, "because they can replay their program and listen to it from various places in the auditorium, checking volume and balance."

"Did things vibrate around the auditorium when you first played this organ?" he was asked. "Yes they did." There were plumbing pipes that jangled inside the walls. Someone had to feel around in the dark crawl spaces and put foam underneath. It took about an hour to fix. "There are still rattles here and there," he said.

Phil Smith is delighted to be the Conservator of this unique instrument. He came on the scene just when the organ was being installed. He would improvise occasionally so that Manuel J. Rosales could hear how a new stop sounded. Sometimes, Frank Gehry or Yasuhisa Toyota would listen, too. "It's wonderful to find organs back in concert halls," he said, "and we need to expose kids to this instrument. Many of them don't go to church anymore, but they should still hear these magnificent sounds."

L TO R: PHILIP SMITH, CONSERVATOR; MANUEL J. ROSALES, TONAL DESIGNER; AND, ED YIM, DIRECTOR OF ARTISTIC PLANNING FOR THE LOS ANGELES PHILHARMONIC AT THAT TIME

FREDERICK SWANN
Organist Emeritus

Frederick Swann had the distinction of playing the inaugural performance on the Walt Disney Concert Hall organ, September 30, 2004 — a fitting honor for a renowned musician. Most satisfying to him was the indication from the audience that two-thirds of them had never attended an organ concert before, and when asked if they would come back there was a resounding affirmation of applause.

JZ/ **You've played so many different organs around the world, what is your reaction to this one?** FS/ It's a great instrument. Each one is unique and has its own sound, depending upon its acoustical environment. It was designed to be used with the orchestra and works superbly in that capacity. It is also good as a solo instrument. All periods of organ literature can be performed effectively on it.

JZ/ **What is your opinion of the acoustics of the hall in regard to the organ?** FS/ The acoustics are probably better for the orchestra. Ideally, an organ requires a minimum of four seconds of reverberation time in order for the sound to mix and 'bloom.' There can be such a thing as too much reverb, but the Walt Disney Concert Hall has a moderate amount.

JZ/ **Did you rehearse using the upper console at all, or just the stage console?** FS/ I used only the stage console. Although the action is more direct at the upper console, it is too difficult to hear balances between divisions. It would require the ears of another organist to help a performer choose registrations that would sound in proper balance to the audience.

JZ/ **Was there enough rehearsal time?** FS/ It was adequate. Most organists desire lots of practice on an organ as unique as this one. However, I was already familiar with the organ due to the time spent in organizing the AGO convention a few months earlier.

JZ/ **Tell me more about your involvement in this convention for the American Guild of Organists?** FS/ Well, as Program Chair I was Robert Tall's right-hand man during the four years in which we prepared for this event. It was a huge undertaking, and we wanted to be sure that everything was in place before the opening — and it was. We were so fortunate to have stunning venues and marvelous new organs, plus 'household name' locations such as The Crystal Cathedral, Hollywood Bowl, the beautiful First Congregational Church (known to have the largest pipe organ in the world), and of course, the new Walt Disney Concert Hall and the new Cathedral of Our Lady of the Angels. Being the first people to hear the Walt Disney Concert Hall organ in our private AGO concert was thrilling. All three organists who performed had special reasons for being there: Cherry Rhodes as a local organist associated with James Hopkins and premiering his commissioned piece; Joseph Adam because of his association with the new organ in the Seattle symphony hall, plus having a Rosales organ in the cathedral where he plays; Robert Parris due to his association with Leo Sowerby and his particular concerto which was featured in the program. This concerto was written for E. Power Biggs, and Robert Parris is the only other organist to have performed it. The Program Committee began with a list of nearly 150 artists from which to choose the final performers for the various programs during this six-day convention. For the Walt Disney Concert Hall venue, the decision was easy, for the reasons listed above.

jz/ **Your performance for the inaugural concert was reviewed by Mark Swed in the LA Times. Do you agree with his opinions?** FS/ Well, he said that he was neither an organist nor an organ authority, but then went on to give his views anyway. At least he was speaking the truth when he wrote that the Willan piece "uses the full resources of the organ." He also said that the "stirring deep pedal tones produced a sonic weight that seemed to anchor the entire building, while the upper diapason notes were clear and warm." He characterized the Baker piece as "trite Christmas caroling" — whereas I chose it for its great beauty and the opportunity to show specific French sounds. The audience loved it. The Dillon piece, *Woodland Flute Call*, was described as "adorable" — but I would put it more in the "trite" category. I included it because it is by a Los Angeles composer, and it allowed me to demonstrate the pajaritos bird warble sound which the audience enjoyed. Mr. Swed even allowed that I played it "with exactly the exquisite grace that it deserved." I selected every piece to show off the various aspects of the organ. As Mr. Swed concluded: "Swann has warmed it up, and it is now ready to roar."

ANATOMY OF THE WALT DISNEY CONCERT HALL PIPE ORGAN

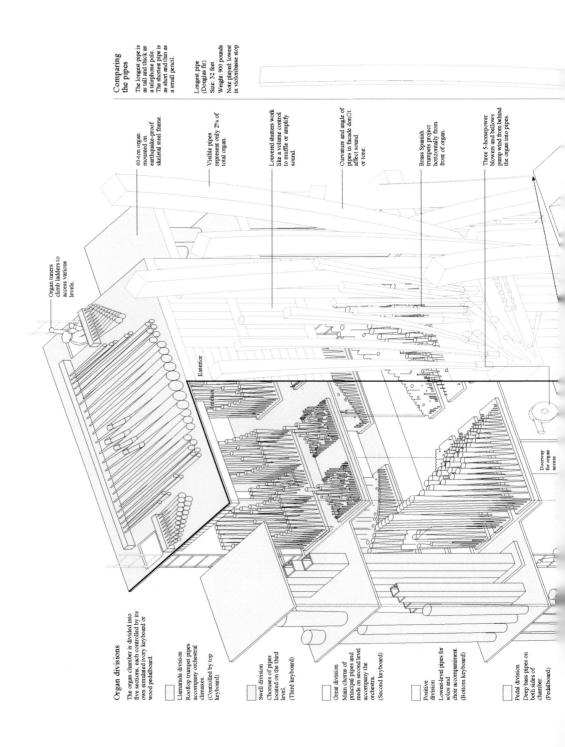

Comparing the pipes

The longest pipe is as tall and thick as a telephone pole. The shortest pipe is as short and thin as a small pencil.

Longest pipe (Douglas fir)
Size: 32 feet
Weight: 900 pounds
Note played: Lowest in violonbasse stop

40-ton organ mounted on earthquake-proof skeletal steel frame.

Visible pipes represent only 2% of total organ.

Louvered shutters work like a volume control to muffle or amplify sound.

Curvature and angle of pipes in facade affect sound or tone.

Brass Spanish trumpets project horizontally from front of organ.

Three 5-horsepower blowers and bellows pump wind from behind the organ into pipes.

Organ tuners climb ladders to access various levels.

Exterior

Interior

Doorway for organ access

Organ divisions

The organ chamber is divided into five sections, each controlled by its own simulated ivory keyboard or wood pedalboard.

Llamarada division
Rooftop trumpet pipes accompany orchestral climaxes.
(Controlled by top keyboard)

Swell division
Choruses of pipes located on the third level.
(Third keyboard)

Great division
Main chorus of principal pipes and reeds on second level accompany the orchestra.
(Second keyboard)

Positive division
Lowest-level pipes for solos and choir accompaniment.
(Bottom keyboard)

Pedal division
Deep bass pipes on both sides of chamber.
(Pedalboard)

Pipe Count

Pajaritos and pitch pipes	5
Wood Façade	51
Metal Façade	73
Wood Inside	239
Metal Inside	5,766
Total Pipes	**6,134**

Facts

The main console is permanently installed at the base of the organ façade — in the "forest of pipes."

The remote console can be moved about the stage and plugged in at four different locations.

There are 80 thumb pistons and 28 toe pistons for setting up preset registrations, and 300 memory levels.

Wind for the organ is supplied by three blowers whose motors total 13.3 horsepower.

The keys on the main console are connected to the pipe valves with a mechanical linkage, or "tracker action."

Both consoles are equipped with electric action to provide for digital recording and playback.

The organ is also equipped with MIDI interface for connection to digital systems. A closed circuit television screen enables the organist at the main console to see the conductor on stage. The organist's bench is raised and lowered with an electric motor.

The wood façade pipes actually "speak" — providing the Violone and Bassoon basses. Behind the façade are metal pipes made of alloys of tin and lead.

The manual keys are covered with simulated ivory and solid ebony.

The pedal boards are made of maple and ebony. The 128 draw-knob controls are hand-lettered on porcelain with solid ebony stems.

The longest pipe is 32 feet, and the heaviest pipe weighs over 800 pounds.

Design, construction and installation of this organ took over 35,000 worker hours.

The voicing and tuning after that took at least 2,000 worker hours. This spectacular pipe organ is designed to be played either as a solo instrument, or with orchestra.

It has a wide dynamic range, from a whispering pianissimo to a thundering fortissimo!

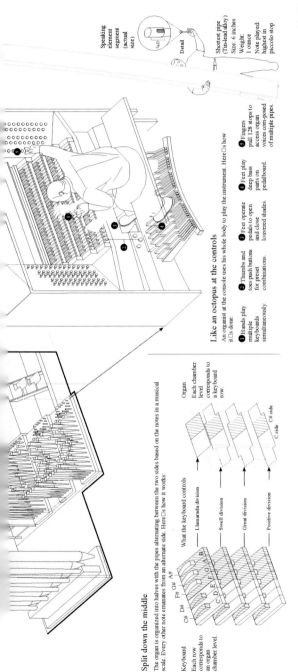

Speaking element segment (actual size)

Detail

Shortest pipe (Tin-lead alloy)
Size: 6 inches
Weight: 1 ounce
Note played: highest in piccolo stop

Like an octopus at the controls

An organist at the console uses his whole body to play the instrument. Here's how it's done:

1. Hands play multiple keyboards simultaneously.
2. Thumbs and toes push buttons for preset combinations.
3. Feet operate pedals to open and close louvered shades.
4. Feet play deep bass parts on pedalboard.
5. Fingers pull 128 stops to access organ voices composed of multiple pipes.

Split down the middle

The organ is organized into halves with the pipes alternating between the two sides based on the notes in a musical scale. Every other note emanates from an alternate side. Here's how it works:

Keyboard
Each row corresponds to an organ chamber level.

What the keyboard controls
— Llaurarala division
— Swell division
— Great division
— Positive division

Organ
Each chamber level corresponds to a keyboard row.

C# side
C side

C# D# F# G# A#
C D E F G A B

THE ORGAN'S PUBLIC DEBUT

The public debut of the new organ came on September 30, 2004,
and featured the highly-acclaimed organist Frederick Swann.
The eight pieces of music selected for this performance demonstrated
the diverse capabilities of the instrument.

Mathias
Fanfare

Rheinberger
Introduction and Passacaglia
from Organ Sonata, Op. 132, No. 8

Dillon
Woodland Flute Call

Bach
Toccata in F, BWV 540

Mendelssohn
Sonata in F, Op. 65, No. 1

Franck
Pièce héroïque

Baker
Berceuse-Paraphrase

Willan
Introduction, Passacaglia, and Fugue

DEDICATION PLAQUE

Placed over the builders' signatures on the Walt Disney Concert Hall
organ case, this tribute was inspired by the words of G. Donald Harrison
who designed or refurbished many of the largest and finest organs in
the United States.

*"To all who read this, know
that the men and women
whose hearts, minds and
hands constructed this
instrument felt the magnifi-
cence and privilege of this
project and were inspired by
the glory and significance of
this edifice. More than the
mere exhibition of their
skills, this organ is their gift
to the musical community.
Through those who chose
us to build this instrument
an iconic and significant
contribution has been made
to American culture."*

ACKNOWLEDGMENTS

On July 8, 2004, I first heard the magnificent sounds of the Walt Disney Concert Hall pipe organ. From that moment, I felt impelled to relate the story of this enthralling instrument. It has taken over two years to complete the research and writing, but it has enhanced my life. The accomplished people I interviewed graciously shared their time and thoughts, sometimes their homes, in my pursuit of an ever-deepening comprehension of the subject. I am profoundly thankful for their perceptions.

From the beginning, I was encouraged by Dr. Robert Tall, the coordinator of the 2004 National Convention of the American Guild of Organists, who arranged for the first private concert on this spectacular instrument, before its public inauguration. (It was at this event that I first heard the beguiling sounds of the pipes.) He advised me to put together a proposal for my book, and kindly introduced me to several key people. He has served me well as counselor and friend.

I gathered photos and did preliminary research, and then proceeded to create a Power Point proposal for the book. In this effort I had the invaluable assistance of my good friend, Edward Mohr, who patiently led me through the technicalities, and asked penetrating questions which forced me to crystallize my ideas. The resulting audio-visual proposal enabled me to contact prospective publishers with a well-developed concept. Then my longtime friend, Beth McClure — a librarian by profession — suggested the inclusion of a CD to demonstrate the sounds of the organ, and presented some helpful ideas for utilizing the inside cover and flaps of the book. Later, I discovered that a cousin, Katherine Hamor, had actually played the organ during a CalArts event.

Always helpful and courteous, Manuel Rosales (the Tonal Designer, Voicer and Curator of the organ) supplied me with essential information, painstakingly reviewed many pages of text, and freely offered numerous photographs for my use. On many occasions, after concerts, he welcomed my husband and me to the "blower room" backstage and graciously introduced us to celebrated organists.

Through the marvels of this electronic age, I was able to "converse" through countless e-mails with Caspar von Glatter-Götz, whose company in Germany actually built most of the components of this remarkable pipe organ. Our correspondence clarified many details and provided instructive captions for the abundant photographs he sent. His associate, Stefan Stuerzer, spent many hours with me, going over the photos and explaining the process of construction and installation. Much of the book is based upon that information.

I am most grateful, also, for the astute business sense of Jan Moya, the manager of the LA Phil Store at the Walt Disney Concert Hall. Her recommendations helped to shape this book and also led me to Balcony Press, whose publisher Ann Gray, accepted my proposal and formed it into a volume of beauty and substance. I appreciate her willingness to have faith in my idea and to bring it to fruition.

Finally, I am indebted to Jonathan Ambrosino, who not only wrote a lively introduction to this book but supplied me with the title. In an article for The American Organist, April, 2004, he used the phrase "a forest of pipes" to describe the playful façade designed by Frank Gehry. The aptness of the imagery stayed with me.

My continuing thanks go to all those who contributed to this book!

THE CONTRIBUTORS

JONATHAN AMBROSINO

Provides consultation and management of pipe organ projects. Has provided editorial oversight, design, and production of organ-related publications. Freelances on tonal finishing, voicing and restoration. Worked for Austin Organs and Rosales Organ Builders. President of Organ Historical Society 1999–2001.

J. MICHAEL BARONE

Host, Director and Producer of Pipedreams — the only nationally distributed weekly radio program exploring the art of the pipe organ. Employed by Minnesota Public Radio since 1968. Graduate of Oberlin Conservatory with B.A. degree in Music History (organ as applied instrument). Held elected and appointed offices with national and local bodies of the American Guild of Organists and the Organ Historical Society. Numerous honors: AGO President's Award, OHS Distinguished Service Award and ASCAP-Deems Taylor Award.

FRANK O.GEHRY

Born in Toronto, Canada, moved to L.A. in 1940s. Educated at USC and Harvard Graduate School of Design. Awards include: Wolf Prize, Pritzker Architecture Prize, Arnold W. Brunner Memorial Prize, Lillian Gish Award, Praemium Imperiale Award for Architecture (Japan). Three gold medals: American Institute of Architects, Royal Institute of British Architects, American Academy of Arts and Letters. Elected Fellow of American Academy of Arts & Sciences. Trustee of American Academy in Rome.

KEVIN GILCHRIST

Joined the firm of Manuel Rosales in 1977. Most complex project to date is the Disney Hall organ: technical design, pipe scaling, voicing and tonal finishing. First organ builder on West Coast to use Computer Aided Design. Member of American Institute of Organ Builders, American Guild of Organists, and the Organ Historical Society. Has played and examined organs in Spain, France and Germany. Later studied organ and harpsichord, and constructed an Italian-style virginal.

CASPAR von GLATTER-GÖTZ

Co-founder of Glatter-Götz Orgelbau, the company selected to build and install the Walt Disney Concert Hall pipe organ. He has decades of experience and a team of organ builders, carpenters, and creative artisans. He believes in modern technology and innovative development. At the time the WDCH organ was built, Glatter-Götz Orgelbau was located in Owingen on Lake Constance, in Southern Germany.

DR. JAMES F. HOPKINS

Professor Emeritus of Music, Thornton School of Music, University of Southern California. Bachelor of Music, USC; Master of Music, Yale; Ph.D., Princeton. Served on faculty at Northwestern University. Compositions include: 7 symphonies, 4 concertos, and other works for orchestra and solo instruments as well as many choral and chamber pieces. Major commissions from National Endowment for the Arts, Pasadena Chamber Orchestra, USC, Orange County Philharmonic Society, and the American Guild of Organists.

JOANNE PEARCE MARTIN

Performs on piano, organ, celesta, harpsichord and synthesizer. Soloist, chamber musician, collaborative and recording artist. Graduate of Curtis Institute of Music, Philadelphia. Appears regularly in LA Philharmonic's Green Umbrella series. Premiered 13 new works with Pacific Serenades. Subject of half-hour feature on The Learning Channel.

CHERRY RHODES

Adjunct Professor of Organ, Thornton School of Music, University of Southern California. Graduate of the Curtis Institute of Music in Philadelphia. Received Fulbright and Rockefeller grants for study in Munich and Paris. First American to win an international organ competition (Munich, 1966). Debut at age 17. Recitals at: Notre Dame Cathedral, Paris; Royal Festival Hall, London; St. Augustin, Vienna; and numerous international festivals throughout Europe. Performed European, American and world premieres of many organ works. Member of the committee to select designer and builder for the Walt Disney Concert Hall pipe organ.

MANUEL J. ROSALES

Born in New York City, raised in Los Angeles. Worked for Schlicker Organ Company in N.Y. and L.A. Established Rosales Organ Builders in 1980 in L.A. Leading consultant in preservation of historic organs. Member of International Society of Organbuilders (ISO). Member of American Institute of Organbuilders (AIO). In his capacity as Curator of the Walt Disney Concert Hall Organ (Opus 24) he is responsible for maintaining the instrument at top quality and lectures about the organ to various groups.

PHILIP ALLEN SMITH

Organist & Director of Music at Wilshire United Methodist Church. Organist & Choir Director for Temple Israel of Hollywood. Teaches organ, piano, and voice. Part of the Price/Smith Duo — trumpet and organ. Bachelor of Arts (Organ) from Spring Arbor College, Michigan. Master of Music (Organ & Church Music) from University of Michigan.

FREDERICK SWANN

National President of the American Guild of Organists. "Most visible organist in the world"— on weekly TV service from Crystal Cathedral, seen by millions in 165 countries. Music Degrees from Northwestern University and Union Theological Seminary — with distinction. Chair of Organ Department, Manhattan School of Music for 10 years. Has performed in all 50 U.S. states, Canada, Asia and Europe. Still performing as a touring recitalist on a limited schedule.

DR. ROBERT TALL

President, Robert Tall & Associates, Inc. Concert organist, recording artist, composer, clinician. For twelve years he served as Principal Organist and Featured Artist at the Hollywood Bowl Easter Sunrise Services. Executive Board Member, Los Angeles Chapter of the American Guild of Organists. National AGO, Director of Committee on National Conventions. Board member, Ruth and Clarence Mader Memorial Scholarship Fund.

CRAIG WEBB

Bachelor of Arts in Architecture, from Princeton University, 1974. Master of Architecture from University of Southern California, 1976. Principal designer at Gehry Partners since 1989, focused intensely on theaters, performance spaces and arts facilities. Has extensive knowledge in this field from the aesthetic, technical and historical viewpoint. Leader on Walt Disney Concert Hall, working closely with Rosales Organ Builders and Glatter-Götz Orgelbau on design and construction.

FOR ADDITIONAL INFORMATION ABOUT THESE INDIVIDUALS, PLEASE GO TO WWW.AFORESTOFPIPES.COM

BACKSTAGE SIGNINGS

The signing of organ cases is an old tradition, dating back at least to the 1700s. Organ builders and musicians sometimes left their names in obscure locations. Many European organ builders have a decorated sheet for the signatures of those who worked on the instrument. At the Walt Disney Concert Hall, builders and organists wrote on the hinged wooden panels of the case.

MICHAEL BARONE, ORGAN CONSULTANT

DAVID HIGGS, ORGANIST

JOANNE PEARCE MARTIN, ORGANIST,
WITH PHILIP SMITH, CONSERVATOR

DIANE BELCHER, ORGANIST, WITH
PHILIP SMITH, CONSERVATOR